For Jack, Zoe, and Beau,
who live completely with love and compassion.

To Theo, for showing us how.

And Justin, for loving me while I learn.

A FEIWEL AND FRIENDS BOOK
An Imprint of Macmillan

Feiwel and Friends books may be purchased for business or promotional use. For information
on bulk purchases, please contact the Macmillan Corporate and Premium Sales Department
at (800) 221-7945 x5442 or by e-mail at specialmarkets@macmillan.com.

Library of Congress Cataloging-in-Publication Data Available

ISBN: 978-1-250-05906-2

Book design by April Ward

Feiwel and Friends logo designed by Filomena Tuosto

First Edition: 2015

3 5 7 9 10 8 6 4 2

mackids.com

Naptime with Theo & Beau

Jessica Shyba

Feiwel and Friends
NEW YORK

Beau is sleepy.

Theo is sleepy.

It must be **naptime!**

Time to **sleep.**

Time to **dream.**

Sleeping on our **backs.**

And on our bellies.

Closer and closer.

Sleeping
right-side
UP.

Or upside down.

Cheek to cheek

and
bottom
to
bottom.

Just right.

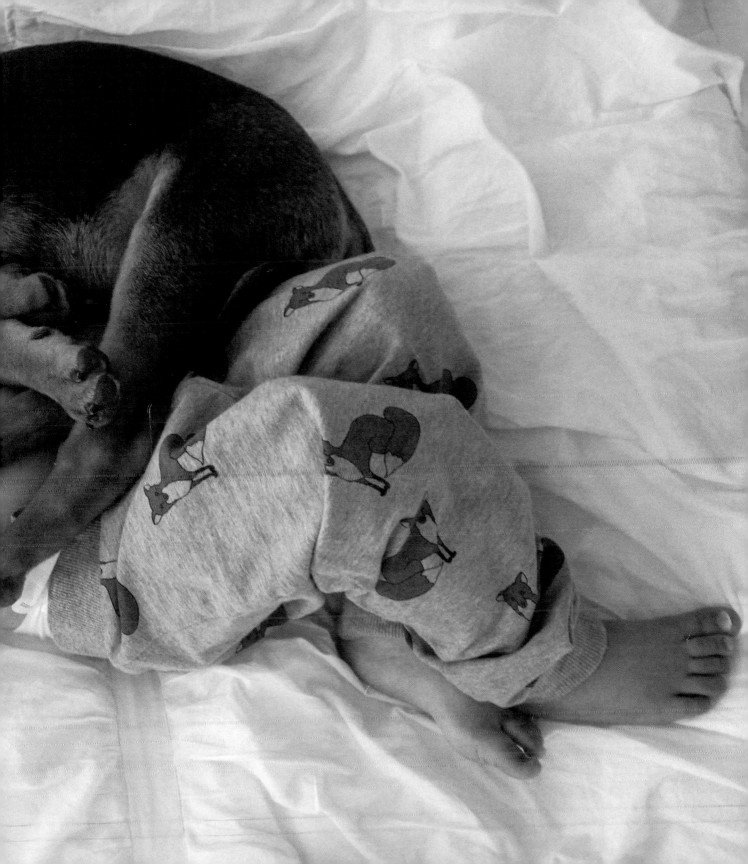

Sleep
tight.

Love you,
Theo.

Love you,
Beau.

Adoption Story

Our dream to get a puppy officially kicked into gear Christmas 2012. We had trekked our three excited kids—Jack (age 5), Zoe (age 4), and Beau (age 1)—twelve blocks to Macy's in Herald Square on a blustery day to meet the wish-granter himself. Jack and Zoe perched themselves on Santa's lap and asked, in unison, for a puppy. My husband Justin and I uneasily gasped in disbelief. We were certain their requests would have been on their Christmas gift lists that we had received from them weeks before! A puppy did not make an appearance on any of those lists.

With a pending move to California and dogs being forbidden in our building in NYC, we were facing a conversation that we had hoped to avoid for at least a year. It was a hard moment for us as parents. We wanted to instill in the kids the idea that having a puppy was a big responsibility—one to be earned—and that a puppy would need attention and love just like we did.

We moved to California in August 2013, and quickly began looking at local animal shelters for a dog to adopt. The children came with us on more than one occasion, and each time we left without a puppy, my heart broke. Justin and I couldn't agree on what kind of dog would be best for our family and the ones we were meeting were too tiny, too hairy, or overly jumpy. We were hoping to find a pup with a mild demeanor and, until then, hadn't been successful. On our fourth visit, we found our puppy tucked together

with his two siblings in the backyard of the Santa Cruz SPCA. Big Bird, as he was named at the shelter, was the shyest of them all, but he bounded instantly into Beau's lap as soon as Beau entered the pen. The look on the puppy's face and the way he responded to the kids so quickly convinced us that we had met our newest family member. We decided to name him Theo, partly because it was my grandfather's name, and partly because it just sounded right.

On his third day home with us, Theo came up to the bedroom as I quietly rocked Beau asleep for his afternoon nap. I was nervous that they'd distract each other, but instead, he crawled right on top of Beau and they both fell asleep immediately. Each day since, Theo meets us at naptime and then waits patiently for Beau to fall asleep. By that time, Theo's also sleepy, so I hoist him onto our bed, and he stumbles over to Beau and plops right down on top of him. And there they sleep, entwined, for at least two hours.

This little ritual of Theo and Beau's has continued daily for months now, and only at naptime. Theo takes turns with the big kids at night, most often with Zoe, waiting for her on her bed at their 7:30pm bedtime. Theo is an incredibly patient pup and while he is plenty rambunctious with Beau, he can be quiet and still, and is very much an old soul with a heart full of love.

I'm not sure how we got so lucky to bring this particularly perfect pup into our lives, but he has changed all of us for the better. There's a reason they call Rescue Dogs their very own breed. They are unique and loving, and I'm so glad Theo chose us.

Jessica Shyba